To Alison

The Undefeated

WITHDRAWN

THE
UNDEFEATED

UNA McCORMACK

A TOM DOHERTY ASSOCIATES BOOK
NEW YORK

This is a work of fiction. All of the characters, organizations, and events portrayed in this novella are either products of the author's imagination or are used fictitiously.

THE UNDEFEATED

Cover art by Chris McGrath
Cover design by Christine Foltzer

Edited by Marco Palmieri

A Tor.com Book
Published by Tom Doherty Associates
175 Fifth Avenue
New York, NY 10010

www.tor.com

Tor® is a registered trademark of
Macmillan Publishing Group, LLC.

ISBN 978-0-7653-9924-3 (ebook)
ISBN 978-0-7653-9925-0 (trade paperback)

First Edition: May 2019

The Undefeated

One

MONICA GREATOREX HAD, in her sixtieth year, resisted acquiring dependents but had (in that easy way we may observe in the rich wherever and whenever we are) accrued considerable wealth without particular effort on her part. Money begot money, and this miraculous alchemy had eased Monica's passage through life, a life which she would be the first to admit had been blessed—with adventure, travel, lovers of all persuasions, and, above all, the liberty to do whatever she chose. Looking back over her six decades, she was satisfied that she had not, on the whole, squandered either her talents or her resources. In her youth she had been glamorous and notorious, making a dazzling match to a writer renowned for his courage and virility; but, seeing herself in danger of being wholly eclipsed by his sun, she ended the union abruptly, remaining the chief (if unadmitted) subject of his prose until the end of his life. After this had come what she called "the wandering years," journeying around the periphery worlds in search of kicks and stories. This was towards the end of the Commonwealth's last big push for expansion, and the sight of a refugee child eating grass transformed Monica's consciousness. She became a warrior with words then, sharp despatches from up and down the front that made her reputation for courage and unorthodoxy. Some credited her with shifting public opinion; Monica herself knew that history was not authored singly and that she had merely been the right person in the right place at the right time. Still, the awards had been pleasant, people's lives had been saved, and an old grudge had been settled.

She enjoyed life in the public eye for many years until she reached her fifties—a dangerous time for a woman—when she was forced to return to old Earth to oversee the decline of her mother and, eventually, the inevitable clearing of a house. Once the necessary formalities were complete, she left that torpid world as quickly as she could, returning to her wandering, pushing ever outwards from the core towards the periphery, in search of something different now—some meaning, perhaps, some form of understanding of the changes she had seen throughout her life, and the changes that were about to come. Her writing by now was long-form, less amenable to the swift attention spans of her former audiences. Commissions and engagements had disappeared and she suspected that many people assumed she was dead. She thought that she was never more alive—pushing out towards the edge, towards freedom, but eventually she admitted that her course, while slow and erratic, had been drawing her ever nearer to the source of all her wandering: Sienna, the world where she had been born, and from which she had been abruptly transplanted after her father's death.

Her haphazard journey had so far taken the best part of three years. She was in no particular hurry, although she was aware that events might overtake her. Still, for the moment she was content to observe, at first hand, the differences in these places since the travels of her early womanhood. Not all of them had resisted the Commonwealth's expansion, accepting it as inevitable, and they had come through those years more or less intact. Even in those which had insisted upon their right to self-determination there was by now little evidence of those years of disruption. All across the periphery worlds, there had been a great levelling, exactly as the Commonwealth promised. There were schools, and hospitals, and business centres, and great towers of glass and steel, and if anything of particular interest or value had been lost in this explosion of creation, there was little sign of its ruins. Except perhaps here and there, in a quiet backwater, where Monica saw old people, in old buildings, clinging to old customs as their worlds decayed about them, their descendants long gone. She would stay awhile, observing, and then would be gone. Dimly, at the back of her mind, she felt the first stirrings of a book forming about these dying worlds, but she committed nothing to paper. It was hard to write, at this time, when nothing about the future was certain.

So her voyage continued, from comfortable long-haul liner to comfortable long-term let, and whenever her companion, Gale, hinted discreetly that perhaps they might think of finishing this trip and returning to the central worlds, she would move them on in the opposite direction. These hints had become more frequent in the past few weeks and, had this not been Gale, and had Gale not been jenjer, Monica might have called them "urgent." She was aware (How could she not be?) that many other people were now in transit, and that she and Gale were travelling against the general tide. But she was not finished. Not yet.

Their next stop was Meridian Station, and she knew that Gale had the impression that this would be as far as they would go. But from Meridian you could perhaps get passage to Sienna, and on Sienna . . . Well, what exactly would be waiting for her there? Monica was not sure. Over the past few weeks, as Sienna drew closer, she had been revisiting her earliest memories. She remembered her mother, cool and distant, and her father, source of authority and some affection, but no less distant. She remembered the sun upon old stones, and inexorable water, stretching beyond the horizon, the limitless expanse of the lake. She remembered the shock; but she knew she had forgotten the whole. It all happened many years ago, of course, and more had been forgotten than Monica as yet realised, but memory abhors a vacuum, and pulls that way, pulls and pulls. The river of history bends towards restitution.

Cushioned in her quarters, Monica did not feel the liner dock at Meridian, and it was not until the jenjer steward politely knocked on the door of their berth that they were aware that they had arrived. Gale, who had been sitting beside her, rose up, silently. She watched him twitch his collar and cuffs in a habitual gesture which did not, by law, entirely conceal the indigo marks around his wrists and neck. His bond had been costly, but Monica was used to expensive things. He was high functioning; he was handsome, too, decorative, which pleased her. She liked expensive, beautiful things. When he and the steward finished organising the baggage, he offered his hand to help Monica to her feet. "Ma'am," he murmured.

"I don't think we'll stop here long," she said, and she felt his hand relax, a very little, until she went on. "We'll book passage to Sienna as soon as we can."

She observed no new tension, no anger, indeed no sign at all that he was disturbed by this news. He was, after all, very costly. "Of course," he said. "Of course."

. . .

At Meridian Station, it became impossible to deny that everyone else was going the other way. The station was busy—no, frantic—although not yet with the pitiful desperation that Monica had seen in the many transit camps from which she had reported in her glory days. Many of the people here were greatly invested in showing that this was a temporary arrangement and that they would soon be returning this way, bringing their possessions back with them. A winter holiday, perhaps, or spending a few years on the central worlds for the sake of the children's education . . . Anything other than admit that this was a one-way ticket. Was this for the benefit of observers, or for the benefit of themselves? Monica sensed that it was a little of both.

She watched them with professional interest. She drew word-sketches in her mind, little thumbnails that would enliven a larger piece of writing, more out of habit than any expectation that they might see print. The fretting mother; the blustering father; the pale bewildered child who, white-knuckled, clutched some beloved object or adult hand. She saw from the quality of their possessions that these people were the ones with options: they would have other, safer homes, on other, safer worlds (if such a place existed), and could afford to make the long journeys. The poor (and even in the Commonwealth, there were poor people) would follow later, she guessed, carrying much less and going gratefully wherever the troops told them. She saw few jenjer, of course, and was curious to see how people managed with that support absent. Every so often she allowed herself to wonder where they all were. Had they been left behind to take their chances? Had they seized the moment and gone? Or had some preemptive action been taken against them? Gale had also noticed their glaring absence and had attracted some thinly veiled hostility: sharp angry glances; the occasional muttered curse. On the surface he was unruffled, but she promised herself that they would not remain here very long, and even felt a little proud at her sensitivity.

Still, they were here for a few days at least, so she took rooms in the habitat section. This was done with more ease than one might have expected from the crush of bodies filling the embarkation hall. She guessed that people wanted to be sure they were at the front of the queue for passage away from the station: this meant camping by the departure gates, not staying in accommodation. The rooms were pleasant enough for a station this far from the core, and she slept well. In the morning, she walked with Gale to the docking section, and was in time to see the dash for the ship departing for Greymouth. Cases and baggage suddenly became nonessential in the scrum for seats. She stayed aloof, an observer, intervening only once when she stepped forwards to delay the advance of a big man who had attracted her attention several times, with his loud voice and bullying ways. She dropped her writing case at his feet, making him stumble as she bent to retrieve it, keeping him there long enough to cost him his seat. The gates closed with him on the wrong side. He turned to her, looking ready to quarrel, and then Gale made his presence felt, and her adversary went on his way, muttering curses.

"Ma'am," Gale murmured, gently moving her on, "this will soon not be safe."

"I agree."

She had seen enough. The situation was already volatile, and as soon as the freighter captains hawking their goods decided that the money on offer was not worth the risk of being this close to the periphery, it would become desperate. Someone would have to come from the core, she thought, although they might have their own problems soon. Everything was changing so very quickly.

For a day or two she thought that perhaps not even money would buy her passage to Sienna, but at last she found a small ship whose pilot had nerves steelier than most, and was still making semi-regular flights there and back. There was cash to be made bringing people up from Sienna, she said, although she hadn't taken someone back there in a while... She studied Monica and Gale with calm curiosity. Her name was Hulme, and she was a type that Monica had seen again and again in her youth, making a living from the troubles of others, but scrupulously, not exploiting them. People wanted to get away, and Hulme asked a fair price to take them, and she put herself in some danger to do so. Nobody knew when the enemy would arrive, after all. But she would gladly take Monica to Sienna, for that fair price. Gale she eyed thoughtfully, but at last shrugged and let him board.

The ship was snug and well maintained. Monica took to her cabin for the start of the journey, resting, and even going so far as to open her files to make a few notes about what she had seen at Meridian. And what had she seen? Pretty much what she expected: people who had realised that their lives were not going to be able to continue, who were hurrying to find a safe harbour. She had seen this before, years ago, during the expansion. Everything changed; nothing changed. Was that the wisdom of old age? To live through the same cycles, over and over again . . . She stopped writing after a line or two, closing the files. Her mind drifted towards Sienna and what she might see there, what might be left after so long. She quickly gave this up as pointless speculation, and went in search of food. As she ate, she found herself subjected to a series of brisk and no-nonsense questions from Hulme, aimed at establishing the purpose of Monica's journey, how long she was intending to stay, and whether or not Monica had the means to get off-world again. Monica's answers to the last two questions were necessarily hazy. She knew that Hulme found her vagueness puzzling, to say the least, but if Monica wanted to fly into uncertainty without clear plans for how she might come back, that was her business. As to the first question: "I grew up on Sienna," Monica said. "I wanted to see it, one last time . . ."

"Before it's gone for good, huh? You've left it a bit late."

Monica smiled. "I suppose so. Yes, perhaps I should have come back sooner."

Hulme, she saw, had one more question. "Your friend . . ."

"Gale."

"Gale. How are you planning to keep him supplied while you're down there?"

Monica blinked. The high functioning of jenjer, and their longevity, came at a cost to their metabolism, and this required regular and expensive medication, but this was something she never discussed with Gale. It would have been intrusive; more than that, it would have been tasteless. She made sure that the money was there, and he saw to his needs as he saw to hers, and she did not trouble herself. Hulme, seeing she had no answer, moved on; it was Monica's business, after all. "I guess I could always come and get you," she said. "But don't leave it too long. At some point, well . . ." She shrugged. "I can't stay in this neck of the woods forever. If they're coming . . ."

She was the first person Monica had heard say it out loud, and even she hesitated to admit the enormity. *If they're coming . . .* But they were coming, weren't they? There was no doubt of that. Somehow, over the long years, enough of them had got away, and nurtured their fury, and now they were coming . . .

"Well," said Hulme. "You know your own business. But there's not much left on Sienna, and as for your friend . . ." She shook her head. "You might want to think carefully about how far you can reasonably take him."

Monica heard, but with no answer, she deferred the matter to another day.

. . .

Hulme delivered them to Sienna's main spaceport, and

left them behind briskly and without a second look. Monica's last sight of her was Hulme making a deal to take someone back to Meridian. Would she make any more trips back here? Or would she cut her losses now and go? Where would she go to? Where could any of them go? The core was well defended, but she sensed that would not matter to the people who were coming. They would not stop until they had justice.

Sienna, once upon a time, had been strategically significant. The largest in a loose federation of trading partner worlds, it had been proudly independent, and clear in its ambitions to remain so. It exulted in its difference: different measurements, different documents, even conducting its affairs in three different languages. But after it was swallowed up, that significance dwindled. No longer a bridgehead to further expansion, it became simply one of many peripheral worlds within a larger union. Arriving in the capital for the first time in half a century, Monica saw that its fall had been more wounding than in other places. Smaller worlds made the switch to the Commonwealth much more smoothly, substituting one master for another. Places like Sienna, resenting the yoke, chafed against it, thereby losing influence and opportunity. With Sienna's reputation for intransigence (churlishness, some said), the dealmakers of the Commonwealth looked elsewhere to exploit the opportunities in this new region. Sienna's capital retained its old looks, but much faded. No glass and steel, but the old white brick and adobe, decaying slowly under the sun. The old government buildings, which had seemed so glamorous to her when she had last passed this way, aged twelve, now seemed small, parochial, and tumbledown. She suspected they had been this way, even all those years ago.

They found a small hotel that was glad of the guests, and Monica, understanding that the money would be used to take the family to Meridian, quietly doubled the price, ensuring excellent service and embarrassing gratitude. In the afternoon, she rested in her room, white curtains drawn against the light. Gale went out on an errand (to secure what he needed, she assumed, but did not, of course, ask); when he returned he was considerably more cheerful, and he brought with him the information that he had hired a driver to take them out to Torello.

Torello . . . Hearing the name, from someone else's lips, both thrilled and saddened her. Who remembered the place now, she wondered, other than her? Was there anyone still alive who had lived there, known its beautiful houses and gardens, or seen the women in their dresses and the men, handsome and rich, dancing in the lamplight? Who was there left who had walked along the esplanade, and taken the path that led along the water's edge? Who had sat and looked out across that great empty expanse, the deep vast water of the lake? Torello, its way of life, its people, had died nearly fifty years ago. The wider world had changed beyond recognition, and was about to change again. Nobody remembered, and Monica did not remember everything. Not yet.

The driver, when he arrived, was curious about their destination too. "I've never been there," he said. "Is there anything even left there?"

"That's what I'm going to find out," said Monica.

"How do you know about the place?" he said. "I doubt there are many people in the capital who remember it. Just some of the locals."

"I *am* local," she said. "I grew up there."

He whistled. Torello had meant money, once upon a time; real, serious money, of a kind that brought obedience. She sensed a new deference in the way he spoke to her from here on, and he turned out to be a talker. Monica was content to listen. He was cheerful, too, and well disposed towards them: the money from this trip (after Monica's adjustments to his fee) would pay for his passage off Sienna, and take him a good way in towards the core. He talked extensively about what he would do there (much the same as he did here, but with a better vehicle and more prospects: people on the periphery sometimes had an inflated view of what the Commonwealth had to offer them, but then there had been a great deal of propaganda in that direction). After a while, he ran out of topics and put on some music. Gale, who was sleeping, did not wake, but slept on, as if in a regenerative mode. Monica, studying his face, pondered whether she saw new shadows there. He had never had a day's sickness (his documentation showed that), but they were outside the realms of the everyday now. She sighed and looked out of the window. The sun was setting, violently.

"Hey," the driver said, quietly. "What are your plans?"

"My plans?"

"Only, I'm not intending to stick around up there, you know. Straight back for me. It's a long way out and we don't know when . . ." In the mirror, she saw his eyes lift and dart fearfully at Gale. "They're coming, you know," he said quietly. "Coming for us. He won't be protection."

"I don't expect he will."

"You're not frightened?"

She thought about that. No, she thought, she wasn't frightened. The threat was so abstract, so huge—and, to some extent, so unverified—that she had not allowed it to affect her. This, she imagined, was how people on old Earth must have lived with the bomb, or with the thought of catastrophic climate change. What could one do other than what one always did, day by day, and put the coming apocalypse out of one's mind.

"Tell me," she said, genuinely curious, "what makes

you think they'll stop at the periphery?" This was something she had not understood about all these flights. Where did people think they were going? Where did they think they could go, to get away? "What makes you think they won't just press on?"

She saw, from his eyes, that he hadn't thought about that—and the idea suddenly struck him in all its enormity. She saw his face pass from unknowingness to full understanding, and then fear, and then, inevitably, onwards into denial.

He shook his head. "It won't come to that," he said. "The government won't let it."

The government. One could not argue with that, so Monica fell silent. They drove on. Night fell. Monica dozed.

She woke as they bumped over the bridge that led into town. Outside it was full dark, but Monica knew, as one does at a homecoming, that they were near the place where she had spent her childhood.

The road was not good, and unlit. They drove slowly, Monica murmuring directions. The lights at the front of the car skimmed the space in front of them, and she found this was enough. The memory of the geography was strong. She knew the lake was there rather than seeing it, a great emptiness to their left, with nothing beyond. Slowly, they inched up what had once been the esplanade, and she guessed from small clues that they were drawing near what had been the hotel. That, at least, had still been standing when she last saw it.

"You can stop here," she said, and the driver obeyed. The lights from the side of the car revealed the hotel's wooden portico, the struts once white, but peeling. There had been red roses painted on this, once upon a time. Could she see them still, or was that wishful thinking?

Gale was out and dealing with the bags. The driver stayed in his seat and did not turn off the machine. When the luggage was out, Monica paid him, and the driver looked at her anxiously. "I'm not sure about this."

"It's fine," she said. "I grew up here. I know the place well."

"There's nothing here! There's not been anything here."

"I'll be fine."

He sighed. He looked beyond her at the dark entrance. His eyes flicked sideways once again at Gale. He shook his head, but there was no point arguing, so he said his goodbyes, and slowly turned the car. She watched him leave, and, silently, she wished him luck in the days ahead and hoped that the money she had given him would take him to a safe harbour.

With the lights from the car gone, the world around was suddenly very dark. She heard, rather than saw, Gale fumble in his pockets, and then the light on his handheld came on. He held it up in front of them, casting a strange angular light on his features.

"Well," he said. "Here we are."

They had been companions for several years now, his presence constant, but suddenly, in this remote place, Monica was conscious, as never before, of being alone with him. She looked up at the front of the hotel. "Let's start here," she said. "We can go and find the house in the morning."

They went up the steps. The door opened, easily, exactly as she remembered from all those years ago, and she caught her breath at the thought that she was here again, in Torello, the town by the lake, the start of it all. She walked inside, slowly, Gale close behind, holding up the light, moving it from side to side so that Monica caught glimpses of the foyer beyond.

"This hotel had a superb reputation," she said. "Small, but very exclusive. People came from the capital to eat in the restaurant. It only seated ten people."

"A different world," Gale said, from behind her.

"Indeed." She moved slowly towards the desk. The bell was still there. She wondered what would happen if she rang it.

She didn't get the chance. She felt Gale's hand upon her shoulder, pulling her aside, and then, a split second later, a shot rang out, overhead. Home, she thought; I'm home.

• • •

The lights went on. Monica, lying awkwardly on her side, on the floor, heard footsteps come slowly towards them. She turned her head to see who it was, pushing away Gale's restraining hand.

An old man looked down at her. He was holding a rifle, and his hands were shaking.

"Fabien?" she said.

He stared down. He blinked. "Monnie?"

She laughed. "I haven't heard that name in a while."

He put the gun down, reached out his hand, and helped her to her feet. "What are you doing here?"

"I could ask you the same thing. I thought the town had been abandoned."

"It was, more or less. A few stayed on." He stopped, and looked at Gale. "Who's this?"

Monica collected herself. "Oh, forgive me. This is Gale. Gale, this is Fabien. His father owned the hotel when I was a girl, and he ran the place . . ." She did the sums. He must be seventy-five, at least. "Fabien, have you been here all these years?"

He laughed, shook his head. "Good God, Monnie, no! There's been nobody here ten years or more. I came back at the start of the month to see to a few things . . ." He eyed Gale again, more suspiciously this time. Monica didn't press. Who knew what family secrets Fabien had to attend to? She had come back, after all, hadn't she?

"Well," she said. "Never mind about that. Do you have any rooms?"

He burst out laughing. "It's a while since anyone has stayed! But hospitality is hospitality. You're welcome to spend the night here—there really isn't anywhere else to stay in town these days." He looked round at the disarray. "I won't charge you the full rate."

He brushed himself down—he was dapper, rather elegant, with short white hair—and took his place behind the desk, clearly relishing the pretence that this was an ordinary hotel, and that the arrival of a guest was a commonplace occurrence.

"And how long are you intending to stay, ma'am?" he said.

"I haven't decided yet."

He gave her an apologetic look. "I should tell you, Monnie—I'm not going to be here by the end of the week. I'm leaving for the core."

"You might want to go sooner if you can," Monica said. "Meridian Station is nearing crisis. Don't assume you'll find a flight, even if you're able to offer a substantial sum."

"I have private means," he said, with a shrug.

The rooms were ruins, of course, but he found her one less dishevelled than the rest, with the windows more or less intact, and he even rustled up some clean-ish linen from somewhere. The art of the hotelier, she thought; to find comfort where it was comfortless. Gale took the room beside her, and made himself a bed of sorts from an old mattress, taking down curtains from other rooms to use as covers. Fabien found her supper, too, and they ate together. With a light touch, she caught him up with her life (although he already knew the broad parameters: she had been quite famous at one time), and he filled her in on what he had done with the long years. A move to the core; a small hotel on a pleasant and exclusive island; a seafood restaurant—he seemed to have re-created as much of Torello as he could, and led a largely blameless life.

"Can I ask what brought you here?" he said at last.

"Family business," she said, leaving him to make up his own mind about that. Perhaps there was some money locked here that she needed to release before Sienna was lost. She saw him wondering, but he didn't ask.

"And how do you intend to get away?"

She smiled and winked at him. "Private means."

Shortly after this, she took her leave and went to bed. He was not there in the morning (neither was Gale), although breakfast had been left out for her: packaged and preserved supplies, but filling and tasty enough. When she was done, she went out.

Her first sight was the lake, of course, directly opposite the hotel entrance, huge and still and foreboding. She turned her face away. It was the very cusp of spring, a crisp day before the solstice, the sun bright, and the rustle of life startling amidst the ruins. Humans come and go, she thought, running from the mess they'd made, leaving it behind them, but after they'd turned tail and slunk away, life went on.

She walked out onto the main road, and along the esplanade. There had been no attempt to rebuild—there would not have been the means—and many of the buildings were sad wrecks. From their skeletons, she picked out businesses that she had once known: all closed, and unlikely to be reopened, the money gone elsewhere. When the stores ended, the town houses began, empty and tumbledown, silent and childless when once they had been filled for summer family holidays. A permanent off-season, she thought. Eventually what was left of the walls would fall, and the plants would reclaim the land, and perhaps, one day, when whatever events were about to overtake them were done, and consigned to history, people—human or jenjer—might come back here, and poke around the old stones, and wonder about the lives that had been lived here.

As the main road became the lane that led up the hill, she stopped walking and turned to take a view of the lake. The water was still and blue. She closed her eyes, and pretended for a moment that the town was still alive with the people she had known as a child, leading that old, glamorous, isolated life, all that she had known, once upon a time. Her mother had not liked it here, comparing the place unfavourably with old Venice. Her mother had talked about old Earth a great deal, regretting this move out to the periphery, regretting the marriage, and, surely, the child. Monica did not visit Venice until much later in life, and found that memory had miscast it. Beneath the reconstructions, she had smelled something stinking, rotten, and decayed. Here . . . She breathed the spring air. It tasted clear and fresh. But then the humans had been long gone.

She walked on up the road and, at length, came to the walls that marked the boundary of her childhood home. She reached the big gates (they were locked) and looked through the railings at the building beyond. People often said that their childhood homes seemed smaller when they visited them again, but Monica had never been a fanciful child, and had made a career from precision of observation. The house looked much as she remembered, but old, old . . . Overgrown, with bits of the roof down. She tested the gate, but nothing gave, and she felt no desire to break through. Would she see anything to her benefit, scrabbling through the ruins? Everything of substance had been removed years ago, when she and her mother had left. Nothing that mattered remained.

She turned and walked back down the lane. Just beyond the boundaries of her old home, she found the entrance to a quiet pathway that meandered down from the hills into town, following the contours of the lake. The sun grew steadily warmer, and she felt the makings of a headache. Back at the hotel, however, she girded herself to go and look at the pool. It was empty, of course, containing only puddles and damp leaves, debris, but Gale was there, sitting on a deck chair, his eyes shut. He looked very tired. She wondered whether he had been rationing his medication: she wondered whether that was a thing he was able to do. Strange, these lacunae in her information, like not knowing how a light worked, but trusting that the switch would deliver what you wanted. She pondered what she should do. She could not ask, and he would not say. There was no language in which to discuss these things; no language between human and jenjer.

She stepped forwards, lightly. Gale opened his eyes. "Do you know," she said, "that the last time I saw my father, he was in that pool."

He didn't reply. He knew that Monica's father had died when she was a child, but he didn't know how, and he would not ask.

"Are we staying?" he said, anxiously.

"Yes," she said. "For a little while."

He closed his eyes again. Monica turned and walked back inside. Fabien was standing by the windows, looking out. As Monica approached, he nodded towards Gale.

"He's jenjer, isn't he?"

"Yes," she said. "Is that a problem?"

He shook his head. "Not for me. I'll be gone the day after tomorrow." He looked straight at her. "There'll be just the two of you here."

"Gale wouldn't hurt me."

"Things have changed."

"He wouldn't hurt me." Even as she said it, she wondered.

· · ·

That night, she slept like the dead. The next day, waking late and queasy, she remained in the hotel, venturing out only in the afternoon to stand and look out across the lake. Had this been a terrible mistake? She had not put pen to paper—but had she really expected to? Would she ever write anything again? She saw nothing of Gale, but his presence was everywhere: her bed was made, and her clothes, pressed, hung in the wardrobe. That evening, she ate with Fabien, and they listened to news from Meridian Station, where there had been a riot, and shots fired. After a little while, he turned it off. They sat in silence for a while. She watched him pass through numerous agonies about whether or not to press her about her decision to stay behind. In the end, discretion won out, and he found some music from the old days, and they spent the evening listening to it.

The following afternoon he left. That morning he took her around the building, showing her how everything worked, and revealing his stores of food, enough to keep her and Gale for about a month.

"There's nothing fresh," he said, and again he seemed about to press her to leave, but did not find the words. Only as he prowled around the front of the building, waiting to depart, did he ask her explicitly to come with him.

"There'll be nothing coming this way again," he said. "I don't know how much longer there'll be a way out of the capital—"

"I'm not ready to go yet."

"But what are you *doing* here, Monnie? You've seen the house now! It's a ruin! There's nothing left!"

She looked out across the lake. There were memories, of course, but even these she was not quite ready to examine in full, not yet . . . And there was something else, too: that desire to see at first hand what was coming, what changes would come when they arrived . . .

"I'm worried about leaving you alone," he said.

"Gale is here."

"That's partly what I meant."

She cut him off with a shake of her head. He muttered something beneath his breath, but clearly he was giving her up as a lost cause. He was gone within the hour, a small swift flyer descending onto the square, taking him up and out within minutes. She wished him luck, wherever he went; wished him a safe harbour, if such a thing were possible. She thought, as she watched his flyer become a small dot in the sky, that he should have stayed. They could have sat here, listening to the old tunes, quite comfortable as the world ended.

She went back to her room and slept. When she woke, dusk was rapidly approaching. She wandered around the bare rooms, stopping here and there to straighten a picture or wipe away dust. There was no sign of Gale. She sat outside, staring at the pool, a shawl wrapped around her. She was startled from her trance by a quiet cough. She turned and saw Gale, tall and still, standing behind her.

She tightened the shawl around her.

"Come inside," he said. "I've made supper."

She rose, and followed him into the dining room. He had lit candles. They sat and ate together, as they had done on many flights. Music was playing, which gave them an excuse not to speak. He had done a good job with the food, which was more than palatable, and which was one of the things she had paid for when she bought his bond. She looked out at the pool and thought about her father. Eventually, she said, "There used to be a pharmacy on the main street. A block along from here. That was fifty years ago and there's hardly anything standing. But who knows what you might find inside?"

He stood up at once and left. She watched the candles for a while, and then got up herself and went outside. The evening was turning chill, but the night sky and the sharp scent of the early flowers brought back in a sudden rush memory of her childhood, memories of her father and the last summer before his death. Tentatively, she touched these memories, beginning to disinter them and to bring them out into the unforgiving light.

Two

SHE TURNED TWELVE AT the end of that summer. By then they were in flight. She recalled a cake with the wrong number of candles, presented as an afterthought somewhere beyond Meridian Station (her mother always relied on someone else to do the date conversions). She could not remember gifts, but she assumed that there were (there were always many gifts, before and after), or the promise of gifts, but she could not remember anything particular. The previous year there had been the tent, her father's choice; the following year brought rubies, picked out by her mother, and the end of any chance of adventure, at least until the arrival of the famous writer, and their elopement.

But at the start of that summer they all still lived where Monica had always lived, in the big house along the road to the town by the lake. She had been Monnie then, not Monica, beloved only child, fiercely adored by her father, absently spoiled by her mother. She was young for her age, but nevertheless beginning to realise, dimly, that the life that she led on Torello was

strange, pampered, and rather feral. Money was plenti-
ful; structure less so. Her father, who would have been
confident educating a boy, was vaguer on girls, but
thought well of fresh air and self-direction. Monnie
mostly kept herself occupied—walking, swimming,
riding, reading—and occasionally submitting to her
mother's demands for a demure and decorative daughter. Once a week, perhaps, she was subjected to the
attentions of a jenjer maid, to be combed, untangled,
dolled up, and then sat quietly at dinner until her father bored of his wife's conversation and went to his library.

But rumours of change were already in the air. Since
the winter, her mother had been talking about schools,
off-world, preferably back in the Commonwealth, in the
core. Her father, who could see only the child (Monica
suspected that, had he lived, he would only ever have
seen the child), wanted to keep her at home. Monnie herself had no desire to be anywhere else, and was willingly
complicit in her own exclusion from the wider world.
Later, she realised that her mother had been right (in the
way that stopped clocks are sometimes right), and that
having the run of a remote town (however luxurious)
was no education for anyone. And it seemed that her father was beginning to be persuaded of the need for some
constraints: he had, in the past few months, insisted she

was home before sunset, and had finally agreed with her mother that Monnie should have a tracker put into her.

Monnie, to give her some credit, had grasped that part of the reason for this was the presence in town of the Men. She capitalised them in her mind, and they remained the Men even when she grew older. The Men had arrived midwinter, taking up residence in the Grand Hotel. Her father, in a rare explicit instruction, had forbidden her from going anywhere near them. And yet Monnie knew (because she listened at doors and windows), that he was one of the people who had arranged for them to be here. She knew that her father and his friends were worried, that they had been worried for some time, at least since the death of Mayor Langley, and that these worries had led to these five Men, and their weapons, being installed in the hotel, where day by day, they looked out across Torello rather in the manner of robber barons considering a new demesne. One of them in particular, named Vincenze, stood out: tall, solid, with dark hair and an air of what she would recognise in later life as controlled brutality, waiting for its moment to unleash. He was their leader.

Monnie, at nearly twelve, did not have the tools or knowledge to join the dots, but when Monica was older, writing from the front lines at the height of the Commonwealth's expansion, she saw this pattern repeated many times on independent worlds. By fair means (economic sanctions) and foul (undercover operations), the Commonwealth would begin destabilising a small, independent world. Things would fray. Resources would be pulled back to the main cities, and the more distant towns and settlements were left to fend for themselves. The poor would give up and move on; the rich might pay for a while to be protected. At length, one of two things would happen. These outlying places became so unstable that the chaos would spread to the centre, or else the centre itself could no longer hold, and toppled, taking the townships with it. Either way, everything would crumble, and the Commonwealth moved in, for the good of everyone concerned. Monica saw this again and again, and wrote about it at length, but this time—here, at her home—was her first experience, and she did not see where it all inevitably led. Still, she knew something was not quite normal, and so she did not resist the tracker, although she did resent the intrusion.

(The tracker was still beneath her skin, now, in her sixtieth year, and, standing once again by the empty pool of the Grand Hotel, she pressed her fingers against her left wrist, and found its small square. She wondered whether it was still transmitting, and, if so, who might be listening. She wondered how many others of her age were still out there, carrying the debris of parental paranoia, and whether the duty of care had been handed over, like an old debt passed on from collector to collector. She wondered if someone would come to investigate if her heart suddenly stopped beating, and she decided that, given her current location and the current climate, the answer was probably "no.")

But even with these new intrusions, her everyday life continued much as it had ever done, with plenty of time left to her own devices to wander the woods and the lakeside, coming back to the house when she was tired or hungry to ask the jenjers for whatever she wanted. Most evenings were quiet, but every so often (less so this year), her mother would entertain, or go out to be entertained, and Monnie would watch the jenjers dress her, and listen to her running complaints that she was not in the capital, or, better still, the Commonwealth itself, the core worlds of her childhood and her youth. "Don't make the mistake that I made, Monnie," she would say. "Marry someone who will take you places, who'll take you to see things." (Which Monica did, although she didn't realise she was obeying this injunction at the time; quite the opposite, in fact. Another reason to consider that whole business a mistake.) When the preparations were done, her mother would sweep out of her room, preparing to lay siege to Torello. Monnie would watch guests arrive—if the party was at home—and listen for a while to their laughter and chatter, and then slip out of her bedroom window and go up the hill to look out across the lake. (If the jenjer knew anything about her night-time wandering, they never told.) It was a simple life, and Monnie, quite simply, was ripe for adventure.

That morning—the morning when the visitor arrived—Monnie woke early and went to the kitchens. The jenjer were all there, eating, and someone found her breakfast, and lunch, and packed these up and sent her on her way. Her father was probably awake, but not yet up and about, and her mother did not usually rise before nine. Monnie took the opportunity available to slip away. The house was set a little way back from the lake, but she did not want to remain on their grounds, which were too tame, so she slipped through a hole in the fence that she kept open, and walked on up the hill. She took a well-worn if unofficial path that led steadily upwards, the lake to her right, dipping in and out of view as she walked. After about half an hour, she came to the top of the hill, where she sat and ate her breakfast, and looked out across the water.

Here, Monnie could turn right and see her whole world—the town of Torello and its languid inhabitants—or turn left and see the empty vastness of the lake. Nothing lay beyond Torello, just water and the wilderness. But this morning, sitting looking out, she saw the impossible: a black dot on the horizon, coming closer.

Monnie screwed up her eyes. A boat, yes, small and moving slowly but definitely. Monnie murmured to herself. Where had it come from? The road came into town and ended here, and then there was the lake, and then there was nothing. There was nowhere beyond here, nowhere to come from. But here it was, and it was heading for town.

Monnie jumped to her feet. Visitors were not uncommon—although her mother would certainly welcome more—but that kind of visitor was familiar, and came and left by air. The Men were something new, that was true; but they had come by road, roaring into town in three huge trucks. This? This was entirely new.

She jumped to her feet and began to scramble back down the hill. She caught glimpses of the boat, drawing ever closer to the shore, and from its rate of approach, she thought she could get there before it landed. She snuck through the grounds of the house, and came out onto the road that led into town. Then she ran like the wind, past the four big houses that lay between her father's house and town, and out onto the esplanade, where she broke into a sprint, passing the town houses and the shops and the hotel. She reached the quay just in time to watch the boat make its final approach.

At first Monnie mistook the single passenger for a

man, since she had never met women who looked like this. Her mother's friends were on the whole more perfumed and idle, and she thought of the jenjer as sexless. This person was strong, and active, and capable, but undoubtedly a woman. A woman, travelling alone, in a boat of her own, and landing here, in Torello, without so much as a by your leave.

By now, the visitor had attracted considerable attention, and a crowd of nearly a dozen had gathered near the quay, watching her secure the boat, whispering and muttering to each other. The visitor did not seem to care about the attention she was attracting (something else new, Monnie thought, as her mother, for example, cared more than anything else about the attention she attracted). The crowd, shifting around, began to block her view, and Monnie, slight and slender, slipped through to the front, until she could get a good look again at the visitor. Here she got her next, and her biggest, surprise. As the woman worked to secure the boat, Monnie saw flashes of indigo around her wrists, and, when she looked up, she saw the marks on her temples. This woman was jenjer.

That was something else unheard of, something Monnie had never imagined possible—a jenjer travelling alone, under her own direction. Was that even possible? Their jenjer didn't leave home often: that was where they were meant to be and, as her mother said, heaven knew there was enough for them to be doing. Sure, there were errands into town, but beyond the town? Her father, sometimes, took one with him when he went up to the capital, but to travel alone beyond town was unheard of. Monnie, if pressed, would have said that this was true for all the jenjer in town. But here this one was, alone. Monnie frowned. Who owned her bond? Where were they? This wasn't right. Something would have to be done. Someone ought to be doing something about this.

The crowd gathering along the esplanade seemed to agree with her. But the visitor, untroubled, jumped to shore, and began to walk along the quay. When she reached the esplanade, the crowd parted to let her through, but they were muttering, and whispering, and trying to come to a decision. The visitor barely seemed to notice them. She stopped, briefly, and pulled out a hand-held device, clearly getting her bearings. When she was done, she put the device away and walked, with new purpose, along the esplanade. When the crowd realised that this jenjer—this *jenjer*—was heading towards the hotel, they reached their limit. Someone would have to be sent for. Something would have to be done. Monnie, pushing through, pressed her face against the glass window, and watched. Yes, there she was, at the desk, checking in . . .

The transaction unfolded as if nothing untoward was

happening, as if this were a person, a real person, check-ing into a hotel. (But she wasn't a person, was she? She was jenjer. Jenjer weren't people, not really, not quite.) Monica watched as a short conversation ensued, and the visitor handed over a credit chip, and then she nodded and walked into the hotel, disappearing down the cor-ridor where the lifts would take her to her room. The crowd narrated this to each other: *What's she doing now? What's happening?* After a little while, the hotel manager came out, young Fabien, new to this game and anxious to make a success, facing the crowd's questions with trep-idation and bewilderment. *What? No, she has money. I don't know how she got it! But she's got it. And what can I do? There's no law to stop her staying here. There's* no law.

The crowd did not like these answers, but they were the only ones available. Monnie, hearing their outrage turn into grumbling, slipped away. She was done here. But the visitor—this was entirely new. Free of the crowd, she skipped round the building, entering the hotel via a side door. Her mother wouldn't like this, and she sus-pected that her father wouldn't either, but they weren't here, and, anyway, there was the stupid tracker, wasn't there? They could find her, if they wanted her. But she wasn't going to miss out on seeing any of this.

In the next hour or so, everything changed, for the first time in Monica's life.

• • •

The hotel jenjer paid Monnie no attention as she ghosted her way around the building. She was a familiar figure in the town, generally with access to all areas, in part because people were fond of her, in part because they were afraid of her father. To her great frustration, she could not guess the room where the visitor was staying, and even she didn't dare to sit in a corner of the bar, so she slipped outside and went down to the pool. At the far end were some trees, and she climbed one, taking advantage of the shade and the cover to hide herself away and wait.

She wasn't there very long. After twenty minutes or so, the door leading from the bar swung open, and the visitor came out. She was still wearing her black clothes, but she had taken off the jacket, revealing her bare arms—bare, that is, apart from the distinctive marks around her wrists—bare, and muscled, and strong. Her left hand carried a drink. Her right hand was in her pocket. She stood on the threshold looking around. When her eye fell on the tree where Monnie was sitting, she seemed to pause in order to study the hideaway carefully. Monnie held her breath and didn't move, so that the leaves didn't rustle and give her away. After a moment or two, the visitor shook her head and moved on. She walked along one side of the pool, coming to a row of sun loungers. She lay down on one of these, started to sip her drink. It was orange, like a sunburst, full of ice, and with a rainbow umbrella stuck in it, and as she drank, her whole body seemed to relax.

By this point, Monnie, in her hiding place, was experiencing many complicated and new ideas and emotions. First of all, she was thirsty, and the drink looked cool and nice. But chiefly (an older, more experienced Monica would blush to remember), she was outraged. Jenjer didn't do this. Jenjer shouldn't do this. Jenjer didn't have rights—they had obligations. Their genetic enhancements gave them special gifts—cognition, strength, longevity, wakefulness—but they came at a cost. And citizens—real humans, proper ones, citizens, not genetically engineered—picked up the tab. They paid for the drugs that stopped the jenjer burning out in no time, and that gave them the rights. They *owned* jenjer. That's what jenjer were. Property. Investment. Wealth. They existed to serve, and this woman sitting here, doing nothing, unowned, was *wrong*. Monnie couldn't say why—she just *knew,* and her indignation nearly ran off the scale. She almost called out, *Stop it! Who do you think you are! Don't you have something to do? Get back inside!* Older Monica, walking beside the dry pool fifty years later, would burn with shame at this memory, and try to console herself with the thought of the many suppers that she had shared with Gale, the many drinks she had mixed for him, icy and thirst-quenching.

But Monnie didn't shout out. Because as well as her outrage, she felt something else, a thrill at the sight of this woman sitting here. How ridiculous, she would re-alise later, much later (too late?), that she should be so amazed. Because what, after all, had happened? A woman had walked into a hotel, bought a drink at the bar, and then sat outside to enjoy it. Sat outside alone, and at leisure. Dimly, Monnie was connecting dots, and grasp-ing that while her childhood had allowed many free-doms, the tracker presaged the approach of a new dispensation—an adolescence of being governed, ob-served, and never left alone. So she didn't cry out in in-dignation. She simply sat and watched.

She didn't have to wait long for something to happen. The visitor's drink was not even halfway finished when the Men arrived. Three of them, big and confident, as if they knew already how the next few minutes were going to unfold. (Vincenze wasn't there, Monica recalled; he had sent his lieutenants, she guessed, to deal with this ir-ritant.) They walked to where the visitor was sitting, and positioned themselves around her: one to each side, one at the foot of the lounger, like a screen erected to pre-vent witnesses. Monnie watched them, and looked at the visitor, whose hand, she noticed, was back in her pocket.

A few words were exchanged, which Monnie could not hear. And then?

And then.

An inexperienced writer, when narrating a flurry of shocking and violent events, may simply resort to saying that they pass at a blur. Monica Greatorex, however, was arguably the war correspondent of her generation, specialising in taut prose that marshalled the telling detail and conveyed swift and bloody action, and, even as a child hiding foolishly in a tree while murder took place in front of her, she had not lacked observational skills. Walking by the dry pool, half a century on, she found that even at this late date she easily recalled what happened next. One of the men drew a weapon. Monnie did not see the visitor draw her own weapon, but she heard its cool blaze. The man crumpled to the ground. A split second later, so did one of his colleagues. There was a short silence, and then someone inside the hotel began to scream. This stopped, suddenly and sharply, and silence fell.

The visitor did not stand up. In a clear voice, raised so that spectators could hear, she said to the third man, "That's two of you dealt. Now get out of here. You and the other two. Get out of town."

He backed away, slowly. She tracked his movement with her weapon. At the pool's edge he turned and ran like hell. The visitor stood up. She looked into the hotel, her head cocked to one side as if inviting a response (it did not come). She put away her gun. She looked straight at Monnie and smiled, and then she picked up her drink and went inside.

Monnie slid down from her tree, and she, too, ran like hell, back to the safety of her father's house.

• • •

Not only fear sent Monnie dashing home. Chief amongst her concerns, she had to admit, was that if word got about of what she had seen, then her own freedom was at risk of being severely curtailed. Her parents must never know that she had been there and seen all, and she needed to cover her tracks. Something else sent her running too: she knew that whatever happened next would be decided in her father's house, because that was where all the decisions about Torello were taken these days. Word of events would already have reached her father, and his friends would soon be calling. Monnie wanted to be tucked away where she could watch the action.

She sped along the back road that led out of town, clambering over small walls and hedges, and coming back down to the main road by one of her side routes, just past her father's house. She was back in her own garden within a quarter of an hour. She walked, cool as a cat, across the big lawn, to the dreaded if familiar sound of her mother's hysterics, and a great hue and cry went up when she was spotted: *Where have you been? You are never where you should be! You will be the death of me!* She faked bewilderment, and explained that she had taken a walk along the esplanade first thing and had been up on the rocks. That would account for any sightings of her in town, and was not, in the strictest sense, a lie. Her mother, satisfied that she would not have to play the part of bereaved parent, quickly calmed down and returned inside, leaving Monnie to get on with her business. Big cars were already stopping at the front of the house, and she did not have much time. Quickly, she slipped into one of the narrow access staircases, used only by her and the jenjer, and by these secret routes came out in the upstairs gallery of the library. She lay down on her stomach and watched through the railings.

She was aware that eavesdropping was not her most appealing characteristic, and that her father might well be concerned about how much she heard, but it had started as a game a year or two back, when her father started to have many closed meetings, and it had become habit. She liked to observe people, and it was a talent that would stand her in good stead in her later career, when few people expected the pretty young woman to be wielding such journalistic power. Listening, observing, learning whatever she could—these tendencies were now fixed, although as yet she lacked the ability to synthesise everything she overhead into a full understanding of the situation. That was not entirely a fault of youth: full understanding of everything that had happened in Torello eluded her until very late in life.

There were three of them, plus her father, the usual suspects—O'Reilly, who was something to do with the bank, as far as Monnie understood it; Patrice, the doctor; and Novelle, the father of Fabien, who owned the hotel managed by his son, and large tracts of land around Torello where Commonwealth citizens could sometimes be found, climbing mountains and looking for the thrills that their regulated civilisation could not deliver. These were the men who owned Torello and, indeed, a great deal more around Sienna. Monnie had known these men her whole life: they were regular visitors to her home, her father being a de facto leader among them (he was deputy mayor, in fact, having refused the post itself when it had become empty a few years ago). They came often to this library, their star chamber, not knowing how closely they were watched. As time passed, Monnie had seen their confidence lessen, the lines around their faces become more pronounced. They moved like worried men these days, paced the room, and they did not take their ease. They were seeing money trickle from Sienna, and were anxious that this trickle would become a flood. Their wives, too, were changing (Monnie knew all their wives; they had often been guests here, in happier times), or were gone to the capital and beyond. Their children she had never really known. They had always been back in the capital, at school. Some were even in the Commonwealth itself. The masters of the independent worlds did not eschew the Commonwealth for the sake of it, and it was useful for their offspring to have familiarity with its laws and customs. And the universities were better. By these subtle means—amongst less subtle ones—the Commonwealth extended its influence, blurred the boundaries until they were all but meaningless. Monica would see it many times over the next twenty years.

They took their seats. One of the jenjer supplied them with drinks, then departed, respectfully.

"We have a problem," her father said when the door closed.

O'Reilly, big and powerful, laughed. "You think?"

"Lay off, Michael," said Novelle. "We all agreed to hire them."

"And what have we got for our money? Nothing. All I've seen is five men sit in a bar and get drunk."

"Four," put in Patrice, softly. "Vincenze doesn't drink."

"You can't prove a negative," said Monnie's father. "Besides, have you felt safer walking down the streets the past couple of months? I know I have. No robberies. No assaults."

"Because they were the ones doing all that," said O'Reilly, impatiently. "Arthur, this is a protection racket. We've been paying these men not to kill us. We should have strung them up last autumn."

"And how would we have done that?" said her father. "You're sharp with that rifle, Michael, but could you out-shoot these guys?"

"He can't outshoot a tree," said Novelle.

There were some laughs, and O'Reilly, who had a gen-erous spirit, joined in. "Maybe not, but there are laws—"

"Yes, there are laws," said her father. "But we have no means to enforce them."

"It wasn't like this under the mayor," grumbled O'Reilly. Monnie saw her father's mouth tighten, and felt angry on his behalf. Patrice had also seen it, and inter-vened quietly.

"James Langley was a good mayor, but he also had the benefit of knowing that support would come from the capital."

"You'd think that after all we've paid into the coffers over the years we'd have earned a little loyalty," O'Reilly complained, moving swiftly to this new target, as Patrice had intended.

"The problem," said Patrice, "is that there's no one to send."

They sat and pondered this for a while, and Monnie, too, thought carefully through the implications. Times were hard; she heard this all the time, and although she had felt no material discomfort, she thought she was beginning to understand what was meant. Independence was costly, particularly when your big next-door neighbour was taxing everything you sold so hard that you weren't really breaking even on making it anymore. Monnie, hearing all this discussed, had sometimes wondered whether it might just be easier to join their club—but she wouldn't have dared say anything like that to her father. Sienna born; Sienna bred. He would die before joining the Commonwealth.

"Is it time to give up, do you think?" said Novelle. "Time to pack up and go?" He glanced at Monnie's father. "Just to the capital, I mean."

"I'm not going anywhere," he said. "Torello is my home. I was born here, my father too, his father—and my girl. I'll leave feet first or I won't leave at all."

"That's the spirit," said O'Reilly. "Still, Vincenze isn't going to take this lying down, is he? We paid them not to put the town to the torch, and now someone has come and shot two of them dead. Vincenze won't like that. Humiliating. He'll be back, won't he? For that jenjer girl, if nothing else. And even if he doesn't decide to punish us, I don't fancy being caught in the crossfire."

"That's more or less where we are," Monnie's father said, with a sigh. "I'll add one thing. I had a quiet word with some friends up in the capital."

"And?" said Patrice.

"And it's worse there than you think. One more problem and I think we're all cooked. We've got to keep this local. Keep it private."

"Damn cheek," muttered O'Reilly.

"I can't say either way," said her father. "But they don't want to know until everything is sorted. For better or worse."

"What's your sense, Arthur?" said Patrice. "Do we really stand a chance of seeing the back of the Commoners?"

"Honestly? I don't know. They've got a habit, haven't they, of taking whatever they want—and they want Sienna. Last world in this sector—well, anything left will do what we do. We've stayed solo this long by paying through the nose—but, well, the money runs out eventually, doesn't it? And then what?"

"Then we can't pay the police, and we can't pay to keep the courts running, and people become scared, and they ask the leaders why they're failing and won't anyone come in to help, and there we are," said O'Reilly. "The bloody bastards."

Monica's father smiled. "And there we are. So we're not going to be the ones to give the Commonwealth the excuse. It was bad enough after Langley died. Let's keep this business to ourselves. We're big enough to look after ourselves."

"You might be," said O'Reilly, "but Vincenze is a mean old bastard and he scares the life out of me."

"Our salvation is closer than you think," said Monica's father. He looked around at his colleagues. Patrice got there first, and he said nothing, only laughed, quietly.

O'Reilly got there next. He stared at Monica's father. "You want to hire the *jenjer*?"

"Why not?"

"Because she's jenjer—"

"She's killed two of them already."

"This is insane," said O'Reilly. "They shouldn't be armed. That's the law—"

"They're used as bodyguards all over the Commonwealth—"

"And we're not the damn Commonwealth, remember?"

"I think I can manage to recall that," said Monica's father, calmly. "What do you suggest instead, Michael? What can we do? Nothing is coming from the capital. Any trouble here might be enough to give the Commonwealth the excuse to come in. We need to sort this out, and quickly. If you've got a better idea, I'd like to hear it."

"As it happens," said O'Reilly, "I don't have a better idea."

"Anyone else?"

Novelle and Patrice shook their heads. "This is a big risk," said Patrice. "She's . . . Well, I've never seen anything like it."

"So we're agreed?" said Monnie's father. They all nodded. "I'll ask her," he said.

"What about all our jenjer?" said Novelle. He must own a lot of bonds, Monnie thought, running the hotel, and the lodges, and the various houses around town.

There was a pause. "What do you mean?" said Monica's father.

"I mean that seeing her around town, armed . . . It might be . . ."

"I think," said Monica's father, "that we can leave whatever discipline individual households might need to those households. I think I can safely say that our jenjer would not be unduly affected by seeing her."

Agreement made, the others got up to leave, but Patrice hung around for a quiet word. "There's something troubling me," he said when they were alone. "I have a kind of hunch, and if it's true, then we might have a bigger problem on our hands."

"Go on."

"I don't think she needs medication."

Monnie's father froze. "What?"

"It's a hunch. No, all right, let me be clearer. There's something going on with the jenjer population. I think . . . I think there's some kind of immunity developing to the drugs, or else perhaps someone has found a way to circumvent."

"You mean here on Sienna?"

Patrice shook his head. "I mean everywhere, Arthur."

Monica's father walked over to the door of the library. He opened it, looked out, and then closed it again. "Have you seen anything like that here?"

"Not until today."

Monica's father shook his head.

"If they don't need medicating," said Patrice, "they don't need bonds, and if they don't need bonds . . ."

"Then they're free. To do whatever they like."

Patrice nodded. Monica watched her father run a hand through his hair. "This is beyond me," he said at last. "It's too big. I've got enough to worry about."

"Well, see what you can find out," Patrice said mildly. "Ask her. Or send her to me and I'll ask . . ."

They went out through the door, leaving the room empty. Monnie rolled off her stomach, and went to sit on one of the window seats. She was shivery, she realised, and would later consider whether some of this had been shock. All that girl knew was that something had changed that day in Torello; some balance of power between citizen and jenjer. Was it really possible that they could go about their business in this way—their *own* business, not that of the people who held their bonds? What could that mean? These questions were complicated, and Monnie would not have answers for many years, and not long before the answers overwhelmed them all. In the meantime, she understood something else, something world-changing.

Her father was afraid.

• • •

Later that day, installed once again in her spot upstairs, Monnie watched her father lead the visitor into the library. She could not take her eyes off her: so strong, so confident, moving with ease across the space. She sat down comfortably in the chair that her father offered. "Thanks for the invitation," she said.

"You made something of a first impression. I thought I should make your acquaintance. I'm the deputy mayor."

"The deputy?" The visitor gave an odd smile. "I was surprised not to be arrested."

"Well, perhaps you did us a favour," her father admitted.

"Oh yes?"

"You've probably gathered we've been having a little trouble here."

"Yes, I gathered. It's the same wherever you go. Indy worlds feeling the pressure. Things begin to crack. Next thing you know you're all Commoners like everyone else."

"Well, I'm not keen on that outcome," Monica's father said.

She eyed him coolly. "It's going to happen."

"Not on my watch."

She smiled, again.

"And that's where I think there might be an opening for you?"

Her smile deepened. "And what did you have in mind, Mr. Greatorex?"

"He's coming back. Vincenze. He has two others that we know of, and there might be more. We want someone to see to them."

The visitor began to laugh. "You want me to protect you from the vigilantes that you paid to protect you?"

"Well, you were the one to rile them, Miss . . . I'm sorry, I don't know your name."

"I didn't give one. Sure," she said. "I'll do it."

He blinked. "Sorry?"

"I said I'll do it."

"Well, that's good. Um, about payment—"

She waved a hand. "I'm sure I'll think of some appropriate compensation."

"We could redeem your bond—"

"That's not at issue."

"No?" he frowned. "As a matter of interest, who *does* own your bond?"

"Your guardian angel," she said. "Mr. Greatorex, these are minutiae. I can do what you want done. I'd like to get on."

"All right." But he was going to check this out, Monnie could see. "Anything else you need. Any, er, necessaries?"

"You mean medication?" Her father looked embarrassed. The visitor smiled again. "I can take care of that. I might need some hardware."

"Hardware?"

"Materiel."

"Of course, yes . . . We'll do what we can. It's not exactly easy getting in supplies, at the moment."

"Not at the moment, no."

"I'm sure that will change soon."

Again, that smile. It would never be the same again. He knew it, she knew it, and Monnie was starting to know it too. They were on their own, and even if Sienna stayed independent, this had changed everything. They'd been taken for a ride by a protection racket, and now they were relying on some kind of weird jenjer to save them. They were desperate people, and they would never come back from this.

The visitor stood up, and Monnie's father led her out. Monnie slipped out through the service stairs, passing one of the maids on her way, and went to her own room, where she lay back on the bed, reading. Her father appeared about half an hour later, and sat down beside her on the bed.

"Hey, little girl," he said.

She rolled her eyes.

"Sorry. Hey, Monnie. How are things?"

"They're good."

He reached out to hold her bare feet within his big hands. She put down her book and smiled at him. "Good," he said. "You know, I was thinking that you and your mother should maybe take a trip."

"A trip?"

"To the capital. Maybe on a little further . . ."

"Further? Do you mean to the Commonwealth?"

He was chewing at his lip, which she knew meant he was about to say something he thought she might not like. So she cut in first.

"What would I do there?"

"See some sights. Your mother grew up there, you know."

"Er, yeah, she's mentioned it."

He laughed.

"I don't want to go anywhere," she said. "I'm Torello born and bred. Like you."

His smile was everything she wanted. "All right. You can stay."

Inwardly, she exulted. The most exciting thing ever to happen in Torello. She didn't want to miss it.

"But will you make me a promise?"

"Sure."

"Don't leave the grounds. Not for the next few days."

She pulled up on her elbows. "What? I'll die of boredom!"

"I don't think you can die of that, Monnie."

"But there's nothing to *do*!"

He was caving, she saw. He had come late to fatherhood, and was not equipped to deal with many of its tribulations. And he adored her, and found it hard to say no.

"There's the *tracker*," she said. "You always know where I am—"

"But I might not be able to get help to you, if there's trouble—"

"Where can I go where there'll be trouble? I go to the lake. I go round the lake. There's nobody *there*—"

"All right," he said. "Just, keep away from the hotel."

"Okay."

"Promise?"

"Promise."

"Good girl," he said, and kissed her on the top of the head, and went on his way. She smiled, glad that he was not curtailing her as much as she feared. It was only later in life that she thought perhaps her father had been irresponsible in allowing her to run so wild for so long. Certainly, when the time came, it was a wrench to leave those freedoms behind—although the famous writer had made her wildness the subject of many a short story, and the theme of his fourth, and what some considered his major, novel. The liberties Monnie enjoyed on Torello had their effect well beyond her immediate circle.

. . .

Over the next few days, Monnie followed the visitor everywhere. Priding herself on how well she kept out of sight (how foolish children are, she would think later), she slipped from shadow to shadow, from hideaway to hideaway, watching as the visitor went from building to building. It wasn't a game (she didn't cast herself in the role of spy or private investigator); more the genuine obsession of an adolescent, caught in the blinding frenzy of a first passion. She studied how the visitor moved, unconsciously imitating her economy and precision, and the languid ease with which she treated everyone she met. Precisely what the visitor was doing as she went round town eluded Monnie: she understood from what she had heard that the visitor was "securing the town," but what this might involve was unclear. Each day would start with the visitor walking the length of the esplanade, stopping to study each building, as if checking her memory of the contents and the occupants. After this she took a longer walk, to the edge of town, perhaps, along the road leading back to civilisation, or else down the narrow path that wound some distance around the lake. After this she ate lunch at the hotel, and in the afternoon she slept, by the pool, before a leisurely outdoor supper, and bed.

On the fourth day of this routine, Monnie saw her father in conversation with the visitor (she couldn't get close enough to hear without giving away her presence). Her father looked on the edge of anger; the visitor was relaxed and unperturbed. (Monnie mimicked her nonchalance to the mirror that night, but would never have dared perform it publicly.) After this meeting, the visitor began to visit each building in the town in turn, and various bits of pieces of hardware appeared: defences, Monnie assumed. She followed the visitor everywhere.

She guessed, correctly, that her parents had no idea what she doing. Her father was preoccupied, and her mother had never kept a close watch, outsourcing those responsibilities to the jenjer. Later, however, after her mother died, and she released her companion, she wondered whether the jenjer knew. Were they watching her, this whole time? Did they ever think that she might be in danger from the visitor? Would they have intervened if they thought she was? Or, with her parents oblivious, were they simply curious to see how events would unfold? There was no way that Monica could know now; no way that she could guess what was in their minds at that time. Would she have blamed them maintaining a cool distance? She had been a child, after all. But they . . . Well, they had been jenjer. How must the visitor have seemed to them? What did she mean to them? What did she signify? What promise did she represent? They saw everything that happened in the house—that was their task, after all, that was why they were bonded and treated, to function at excellent levels, to observe and be ready to supply what was needed. Surely they had seen? But they had done nothing.

For a few days, then, the visitor remained around the centre of the town, going from building to building to secure their defences. Then one morning Monnie went down to her usual spot on the esplanade and sat waiting for the visitor to emerge from the hotel. A quarter of an hour passed, and she didn't make an appearance. As the hour drew on, Monnie found herself in a growing state of panic. Where was she? Where had she gone? Had something happened to her? There was nobody she could ask, of course, as questions would alert people to her interest. After almost two hours, Monnie gave up and headed miserably home. She was worried, of course, about the visitor's safety, but for some reason she felt angry, too, as if some unspoken agreement between them had been violated. At the gates she stood looking towards her home. There was nothing to do but go back, she supposed, but then she felt suddenly angry at the new constraints on her. She kicked at the gate, and then broke into a run, sprinting along the road away from town.

She was soon in open country. The trees grew thickly on both sides. After about half a mile, she came to a turnoff on the right, where a narrow road ran up towards the cliffs. She slowed to a walk and went this way. It was wide enough for a single vehicle, and the road was well kept but rarely used. The trees on each side hung over, creating a tunnel-like effect, their leaves and branches interlocking overhead. She had often come this way, pretending, when she was younger, this was a gateway to adventure in distant times and places, but today she could no longer access any of those old stories. This was a path she had often taken, and she knew that it did not lead to anywhere she had not visited before. She thought, briefly, that her father might not like her being so far away, but she had only promised to stay away from the hotel.

She walked slowly, uphill. Eventually the trees thinned, and she came out onto the clifftop. It was a bare patch, functional; here stood the town's main generator, and the town's linkup to the communications grid. The visitor was there, examining this closely. As Monnie drew closer, she looked up.

"Oh," she said. "You." Her lips were slightly apart, and Monnie observed that her teeth were small, precise, and very white. "I'll say this for you, Monica, you're persistent."

Her tone was careless and intensely patronising. Monnie felt the start of a deep and burning blush of shame. She thought she had been so clever and careful, stealing around town, following the visitor like a shadow. Had she known all along? Monnie guessed, from the languid smile on the woman's face, that she had. Confronted with her own delusion, her own childishness, Monnie felt tears well up. Suddenly, she wanted her mother. She ran her thumb, unconsciously, along her wrist, where the tracker was implanted.

She started. The gentle throb, which she had long since learned to ignore, was no longer there. Monnie frowned, and looked down at her wrist. She ran her fingers along the small square embedded there. She looked up, puzzled, and saw the visitor watching her. Then she looked past the visitor's shoulder at the comms linkup. It was silent and unblinking; it wasn't working either. But that would leave the town out of contact with the rest of the world . . . Monnie had an odd image in her mind, of a blanket smothering the town.

The visitor moved closer. Monica looked at her, her mouth forming questions that died on her lips. She stared at the indigo marks around the woman's throat. With a sudden flash of insight she knew that it must be as Patrice had said. This woman was free of the drugs. And a jenjer free of the drugs . . .

Was a danger. Nobody had said this to Monnie, not explicitly, but she knew it as plainly as if it had been encoded some way in her genes. It was her inheritance, after all, the settlement under which she lived, in which jenjer served so that citizens might play. These were the conditions of her possibility, and for a brief second she saw all their workings, and how the safety was illusory.

The visitor was taut as a cat about to leap. Monnie thought how far she was—not just from home, but from anybody whom she could call upon to help. She looked about, furtively at first, and then more desperately, as if she could by wish alone conjure up an escape route, a portal to somewhere else. But such things only happened in the kind of stories which Monnie had abandoned. This danger was real, it was present, and it was happening now.

The visitor stepped forwards. Reaching out, she clasped Monnie's arm, just above the wrist where the tracker was implanted. Monnie tried to shake her off, but the woman gripped harder. "Don't be stupid," she said. "And don't move."

Monnie obeyed. The visitor stared at her. "You like to watch people, don't you? You like to know what's going on."

Monnie nodded.

"Then keep on watching," said the visitor. "There's plenty more to come."

Monnie didn't move. After a moment, the visitor released her arm. "Come on," she said. "I'll see you home."

They walked back down the hill, and soon Monnie felt the gentle familiar pulse of the tracker. She looked down at it, running the thumb of her other hand against it. The visitor didn't miss the movement. "Safe and sound," she said. "Safe as houses."

Eventually they reached the avenue of trees. Monnie said, "I can make my own way back now."

But the visitor said, "I said I'd see you home, and I will."

They walked on. She heard the visitor humming, as if this were a pleasant walk in the countryside. At the gates to her father's property, the visitor stopped, and she watched Monnie walk slowly up to the house.

That evening, Monnie sat in the tree outside her bedroom window and thought, thought hard, perhaps for the first time in her life, but she did not have the resources to understand the depths of her unease. Only now, long after her father's house had fallen to ruin, did she fully understand: in that moment, when the visitor had been considering her fate, she had known what it meant to be alive because of another person's whim. To be entirely in someone else's power.

To be jenjer.

A child cannot articulate these things. An adult can, and must.

. . .

The end came two days later. During this time the mood of the town became more and more anxious. Their worries were not alleviated by the fact that their guardian angel spent most of the time lying by the pool in the sunshine.

Monnie, who kept to the house now, learned about this when her father's friends convened in the library.

"Now *she's* the one taking us for a ride," O'Reilly said. "Have you seen her bar bill?"

"She must have something in mind," said her father. "She was busy all the time last week. If she needs to rest before they arrive, then—"

"Arthur! She's scamming us!"

"What else can we do?" her father cried, and Monnie's heart nearly broke to hear his distress. "There *is* no one else! If you're scared, Michael, then get out of town. Go back to the capital—"

"And get picked off by Vincenze on the road? No thank you—"

"Then *help*. Get your rifle and be ready when she asks for your help."

"This is my *point*," O'Reilly said. "I don't think we'll be asked. I think there's something else going on."

"Then all the more reason to dust that rifle down."

Later, Monnie overheard her mother and her father. Her father, she realised, was trying to reassure her mother. And her mother laughed at him.

"You don't put your trust in jenjer, Arthur. And you certainly don't pay them." She shook her head. "I should never have let you bring me here. I should have gone back to the core years ago."

On the morning when everything changed, news reached the house that the visitor was nowhere to be found. Her room in the hotel was empty. Her boat was gone. Monnie, hearing this news, dashed down into town. It was happening. It was all happening, now, and she wasn't going to miss it. She stood on the esplanade opposite the hotel, keeping her promise. Everyone else was out in the streets too, talking, worrying, trying to find out from each other what was going on. Monica's father came out of the hotel and tried to speak, but he was shouted down.

"We trusted you, Greatorex! We let that jenjer into our houses, our businesses!"

"She's had free room and board for a week!"

"This wouldn't have happened with Langley—"

And then they heard it: the unmistakable roar of engines heading down the road into town. Someone screamed: *They're coming!* And then there was chaos, as people dashed for cover. Monnie took cover in the alley beside the hotel, which was where she saw a big armoured truck power down the road. Two men were hanging out of the windows and firing into the air. One of them was Vincenze. As they passed the Palmer house, he called down to the driver. The truck slowed. Vincenze lowered his rifle, and strafed a line of fire across the shop front. The glass shattered, and then half a second later the whole building blew.

"Sweet Jesus Christ!" Vinceze cried in delight. He had

not expected this. He fired again, this time across the surgery. It blew too. With a whoop of joy, he sent the van off down the main road, he and his companion firing as they went.

Monnie dived through a side door into the hotel. She rushed through, shouting, "Get out! Get out!" and rushed out onto the terrace to find her father. He was there, talking to Novelle.

"She rigged the buildings," Novelle said. "Explosives. So as soon as they shot—well. Here we are. She was meant to be helping us, Arthur!"

"I know," he said. "I know. I was wrong. Have you heard back from the capital?"

"The comms are down," Novelle said. "I can't get through—"

Her father's eyes closed, for a moment. "All right," he said. "We're on our own. But we'll see this through—"

"Greatorex."

Her father turned. Vincenze was there, holding his rifle to him, caressing it like a lover. "How's your day going, man?"

"Go to hell, Vincenze."

"Not yet."

"What more do you want?"

Vincenze smiled. "I want the jenjer girl."

"So do I," her father said. "But she's gone—she's done

your work for you. Why don't you just go?"

"Not liking how your town looks?" Vincenze laughed. "You're finished, Greatorex. You, this town, Sienna. Finished!"

Her father flushed red, and fumbled around for his pistol.

"Daddy!" Monnie shouted. "Don't!"

Her father turned at the sound of her voice. Vincenze fired, once, twice, three times. Her father fell back into the pool, blood-water all around him.

Monica screamed.

A clear shot rang out, and Vincenze crumpled, dead. The other two men scrambled for cover, but too slow. They were both down in seconds, shot through the head.

The visitor was standing on the step, cool as a cat. She walked, slowly, to the side of the pool, and paused to look down at the body of Arthur Greatorex, floating on his back with his eyes wide and startled. She turned her head to survey the scene, her day's work, and she breathed out, and nodded, as if satisfied. And why should she not be satisfied? Vincenze and his band were dead. She had done what she'd said she would do, and more besides. She turned and walked into the hotel and out onto the main road. Monnie followed.

The fires were still blazing. The visitor walked on through the burning town, calmly, and nobody came after her. Nobody except Monnie, stumbling in her wake along the esplanade. She followed her down out of town along the lake path, coming at last to a quiet spot where the visitor's boat was moored. Before she climbed on board, she turned to Monica.

"What do you want, Monica?"

"What do *I* want?" Monnie wiped tears away from her eyes. "What did we ever do to you? What did my father ever do to you?"

The visitor did not reply.

"*Why?*" Monica insisted. "What did *you* want?"

"What do you think?" said the visitor. "What do you think I want? I want justice!"

"And have you got it now? My daddy's dead! Have you got your damn justice?"

The visitor's face was stern and cold. "We've barely started."

She got into her boat and slowly, slowly, slipped away across the lake into ... nothing? No, Monica thought, nearly fifty years later, into the space where the jenjer were gathering, making ready to come back for restitution.

Monnie stayed hidden in this place for some time. When she got back to town, there were men in uniform there, helping the wounded, stopping the fires, bringing aid. She didn't recognise their uniforms, although she would know them well in later years. A unit from the Commonwealth, sent to clear up the mess.

And that was it. A few weeks later, the Senate up in the capital admitted that it could no longer maintain law and order on Sienna, and more Commonwealth troops landed. It took two more years for the formalities to be completed, but that was the end of Sienna. What money that had not already been moved away drifted towards the core; the people who remained lived on handouts. The whole faded into memory. But of course by then Monnie and her mother were long gone.

Monica, at sixty, walked away from the pool into the dead hotel. She had thought many times over the years whether, if she had warned her father about the visitor, he might still be alive. She had tormented herself throughout her teenage years with guilt at his death, and then suppressed the thought, ruthlessly. Now, at this late date, she decided that she had been guilty of nothing more than youth and privilege, and could console herself that she was no longer guilty of one of those crimes.

Three

BARELY A MONTH LATER Monica and her mother were at the capital, taking their leave of Sienna. The estate would take a while to settle, at least as far as Monica understood these things at the time, but there was already money available to make the long journey to the core. Later—much later, in fact, after Monica had seen considerably more of the ways the worlds worked—she realised that this must have come from selling the bonds of their jenjer. Most of these had been her mother's, indisputably, brought with her when she married and went from the core to the periphery, but only one made the trip back—Lucy, her longtime companion. There had been nearly a dozen others, but Monica did not think about them at the time, did not question why they were not coming and where they were going instead.

The realisation came a long time later. A few months after the whole business with the famous writer was concluded (from her perspective at least), Monica found herself drinking shots late one night in the bar of a hotel. She fell to watching the bartender. He was very young and very handsome, and his eyes were the same shade of indigo as the marks on his flesh: a fairly standard adjustment, which naturalised what might otherwise seem like tattoos or a brand. She sat, lazily, rather drunk, chin on her hand, admiring him: his looks, his manner, the whole overall effect. After a little while, he became aware of her watching him, and he turned, slightly, and smiled at her before moving on. That movement did something . . . She remembered, suddenly, the young man who maintained their boat on the lake, with whom she might well have made a stupid mistake had she remained in Torello a year or two longer. She thought, What was his name? And before she could recall (she remembered only a few hours later, just before falling asleep, that he had been called Cory), she wondered, What happened to him? This made her think of the others—the small quiet army who had tended their house and their grounds and their whole way of life—and she pictured them one by one (even if she could not always think of what they had been called), and thought, What happened to them? And: Why did I never think of this before? Her answer came quickly, defensively: Because you were a child. (A child doesn't ask these questions.) Monica finished her drink and went upstairs to bed, where the name returned at last and she fell into deep slumber. (An adult can, and must.)

Young Monnie, as yet unequipped to form such

questions, never mind try to answer them, left Sienna with her grief paramount and her conscience free. They travelled for a while—Monica, her mother, and the companion—her mother saying that this trip, their itinerancy, was good for Monica, a real education, after those long years buried in that backwater. Monica thought of the summer that would be burgeoning in Torello as they travelled further and further away from the only home she had known. For a while, she held two timelines in her head: the one that she was directly experiencing, of luxury liners and in-flight gossip, and the other, more real to her, of what her life would be if everything had remained the same. Reaching the core destroyed this second timeline for good: the vastness of the main conurbation worlds and her mother's palpable relief at reaching "civilisation," was enough to make clear to Monica that Torello was gone for good. She never wasted her time on fantasies, not even as a child.

Besides, the conurbation worlds of the core were beyond imagining, and certainly beyond her mother's rather limited powers of description. Monica was overwhelmed. (She started to think of herself as "Monica" around this time, with her father no longer there to use a diminutive, and her mother generally addressing her to criticise.) But soon the towers of glass and sunlight that were standard for these central worlds became familiar, too familiar, and Monica found herself wondering what all these people found to *do* . . . Everything felt false, superficial, and moving so quickly that people didn't stop to notice how silly it all was. Still, she dutifully trudged round galleries and exhibitions, and stayed out of the way when her mother entertained. This was not as often as her mother would have liked. Money was a constant theme during this time—her father's money was now Monica's money, and she quickly understood that her mother was unable to touch the capital, and that this was a source of great bitterness. But for the first time, Monica watched how money was spent, how quickly, and on what kinds of things. There was about a year of this, during which time her mother accepted fewer and fewer invitations, and talked bitterly about the lack of new clothes. Monica began to wonder, vaguely, whether it was possible for money to dry up, and what might happen in such circumstances. And then, abruptly, the complaints ended. (Monica assumed some settlement had been reached between her mother and the lawyers, and some allowance agreed; when she gained her majority she saw this was indeed the case.) Her mother became cheerful, gregarious, and decisive. The following month Monica was on her way to an exclusive school two worlds away from the capital, while her mother headed in the opposite direction towards old Earth. The companion went with her. Monica travelled alone.

The school was extremely good, and perfectly enjoyable insofar as spending one's adolescence amongst several hundred other bored and secluded teenage girls can be enjoyable. Monica neither liked nor loathed it. Certainly her mother seemed to think that she was getting what she was paying for (although Monica doubted the fees came out of that allowance), praising Monica's new poise and elegance whenever they spoke. Monica's own pleasures from the new environment she kept to herself: the exposure to different people and ideas (they were a fairly homogenous bunch, all told, these scions of the Commonwealth's richest families, but they were all very well read).

She eavesdropped extensively during the first few weeks in the school: learning what to say and not to say, learning how to pass amongst these alien creatures without appearing alien herself. Her unusual background (and reputed vast wealth) went some way to easing her passage. Sometimes, when pressed by friends, she would call up memories of Torello. Her early years on such a distant world, not to mention the death of her father, attracted a certain amount of romanticism which she herself found ludicrous. Still, she was happy to supply stories of her life there, somewhat exoticised, and she discovered her talent for narrative based on the observation of real life. The teachers noticed too and, she later realised, nudged her to make the best of her gifts. Everything else was gloss, and came easily enough, but she worked at writing, privately (since working at something was considered by her peers to be not quite the thing), and with increasing proficiency. In later years, she came to understand too how those teachers had nourished her, in the kinds of texts they put her way, and the risks they took (they were jenjer, after all) in supplying them. But the ground was prepared here for the awakening that her later travels would bring.

During shorter holidays, Monica was encouraged to take up invitations from friends to travel to their homes and estates, but summer was reserved for Earth and her mother. How she came to loathe that old world! A cross between a theme park and a retirement home, she was desperate to get away (and, truth be told, her visits did rather disrupt her mother's diary). But those other holidays, amongst friends and their families, broadened her horizons, not to mention her connections. She was introduced to the old money that had built the Commonwealth. She came to realise that she had been admitted on probation to this circle: her mother's background was impeccable; her father's wealth was from the periphery, but large. On the last holiday before she left school she met the famous writer, twelve years her elder. He was the uncle of one of her friends, and known to hold radical views. He listened to her acerbic asides about their party with mirth and increasing infatuation. He told her she was beautiful and funny. She thought he was clever and that she was in love. The next month, she turned eighteen, acquired full access to her inheritance, and left the school without graduating, skipping off to the spaceport where he was waiting. She sent her mother a short message after the ceremony, and then they were gone, on their first adventure, which he was to recount over and over in various disguises in his books, taking a scruffy freighter the long way round to Clementia, where the Commonwealth had become involved in an unreported border war which had forced half a million people into transit. They stayed in a hotel in the main city and he wrote his despatches as if from the front line.

She was young, and he was not, particularly, and it was great a scandal at the time. She was not pardoned until the following year, when he won his first major award for his reports from Clementia. He was feted up and down the central worlds, and she was a means to access him. After this triumphant return to grace, she took him to old Earth to meet her mother. That visit Monica often fondly recalled as one of the few genuinely happy family occasions of her adult life.

Her mother adored him, of course, since not only was he famous now, but he knew exactly how to treat her, with a faultlessly well-judged combination of deference and flirtation. Monica, somewhat sidelined, nevertheless benefitted from their mutual adoration. She had at last done something right. Her stock rose considerably, and shot up to hitherto uncharted heights when she provided the funds to purchase the apartment in Venice that her mother had set her heart on. That was Monica's zenith. On the flight away from old Earth, onwards to their next adventure, they were sitting in the bar and she thought, just for a second, quickly suppressed, how much he bored her. The divorce, which came after three years, was never forgiven. Never.

• • •

When she made the break, it was abrupt. She left him at Wheeler's Station, depositing him at the bar with some pals. She claimed she was off shopping; and she did go shopping (Monica rarely lied), for passage on the next ship out. It was three weeks before he managed to track her down and make contact. He tried bluster at first, telling her she'd be sorry and back soon, and when he realised that wasn't going to work, he warned her how angry it would make her mother, and when she laughed at this, he cried and begged her to come back to him. She was sad to see this—he set such store by his manliness—but she said goodbye, and he didn't try to contact her again. (He gave up journalism not long after and switched to novels. It didn't do him any harm.)

Now she was free to lead her own life, however she chose, paid for by the money her father had left her, and not yet twenty-five. She went back briefly to the capital, but she understood, from hints dropped by friends, that the divorce was a scandal too far, and that a period of penitence should now be observed. She found that this suited her perfectly well and, furthermore, that she enjoyed being independent immensely. Her inheritance provided so many options that she was almost spoiled for choice. But she could not forget some of things that she had seen on Clementia, even in the relative safety of the main city. (She never denied the impact the famous writer had on her: opening her eyes to the different worlds out there, giving her the means whereby she might have her awakening. She read the books that he read, tried on his politics and found that they fit, and then she pushed herself beyond anything he achieved.) She was pulled back out to the periphery, and she sat in hotel bars on worlds where the Commonwealth was expanding, and she drank with medics who had been on the front lines, and somehow she persuaded them to take this implausible young woman with them next time they went out. And on Tintagel she saw the transit camps, bereft of supplies, and a small boy picking listlessly at some rough tufts of grass. He looked around, furtively, to make sure nobody was watching—but Monica was, as ever, and she saw him shove a handful in his mouth.

Her account of this, written in what would become her trademark clipped unfussy style, shocked the core worlds into action. There had been a general sense there, growing all the time, that perhaps the expansion had gone far enough, and these pushes into more and more distant worlds were stretching things too far, making the borders permeable, allowing people to slip through (both ways). All that this vague sense of unease needed was a focus for moral outrage, and Monica supplied it. Within five years, the expansion was more or less over. Monica knew that she had played only a small part in that, but it had been significant, and she felt a weight lift from her. It was as if some debt had been paid to her father. Sienna's fate had not been forgotten, and a kind of justice had been meted out.

Monica's *Letters from the Front* restored her to the centre of things. On her return to the core worlds she discovered that she was no longer outrageous, but had done something so stellar, so remarkable, that everyone

wanted to know her again. She had fame—on her own
terms, this time—and a career. One unexpected result
of all this was that she became acceptable to her mother
again, who could understand fame, if not the reasons for
Monica achieving it. She travelled extensively throughout this period across the Commonwealth and beyond,
chasing the stories she knew were there, pricking the
conscience of the empire of which she had become an
unwilling subject.

She remained reliably in touch with her mother
throughout this period, although sometimes commissions took her out of reach for long periods of time. She
made a point—and sometimes considerable effort—to
ensure they were able to speak each year on her mother's
birthday, although on one or two occasions she con-
cealed where she was and the conditions in which she
was living. Her mother did not need to see war
zones—they would distress her, and it was better to
maintain the fiction that Monica's work took her close
to danger but not right into the thick of it. Monica suspected her of keeping in touch with the famous writer
for some time after the divorce. Eventually, this contact
dwindled to nothing more than the delivery, signed, of
every one of his first editions as and when they were
published. There was a shelf full of them by the end;
after her mother's death, when she was clearing the apart-

ment, Monica flipped through the last few, finding him unchanged. She had been right to leave, and she was only glad that she had not wasted too much of her precious time with the whole business.

She visited once or twice, but she still found old Earth deadly, and the lifestyle suffocating. She found the sight of her mother increasingly sad: she was using longevity treatments to keep her "beautiful," but not everything can be held back, and if the gene is there, the gene is there. She wondered, sometimes, usually in the company of another sweet lover, whether her mother might be lonely, but reminded herself that she had her friends, and the companion. Still, Monica knew that the summons would come eventually, and that she would answer when it did; that she would go and sit beside her mother and watch her die. The only question was when, and how much freedom remained to her until then.

. . .

Migration had always shaped humanity's presence on old Earth, whether by the plunder of various parts of the planet, or through forced passage, or by moving in search of a better life away from poverty or war. The various diasporas that had sent humanity off to form the Commonwealth were no different: the first settlers trekking to the new worlds; the movement of jenjer to make the expansion of those settlements possible; and, at last, the removal of the left-behind, those too poor to leave the crumbling world with their own resources (since they had none), some of whom wanted a helping hand to get away, others who, finally, had to be removed for their own good when the core worlds made clear that they would no longer pay to maintain the ruins of the family home.

What had not necessarily been predicted was the return of wealth to old Earth. After the planet emptied, it was left to its own devices for a while, the old places becoming like names in a work of fantastical fiction; unreal cities, lost lands, a whole world turned into Atlantis. Eventually someone had the bright idea that all this real estate was waiting there to be exploited and, even better, that the very rich could be persuaded to foot the bill for redevelopment. Rome, Beijing, Jerusalem, Chicago, Machu Picchu: someone would pay for addresses like that. Soon the old places were rebuilt, more or less; carefully constructed enclaves for the super-rich. Monica suspected that living here was well beyond her mother's means, but the querulous nature of the old woman's voice whenever she touched upon this question was enough for Monica simply to make a few private enquiries and then adjust the allowance accordingly. Thank

God, she thought, that her father had settled the money directly on her: her mother would have burned through the whole fortune in a matter of years.

The first few years her mother lived in London, but she didn't like the weather and, once the famous writer was part of the family, the choosing of a new address was the chief topic of conversation between him and her mother. Their visits would coincide with trips exploring various places, and culminating in one of his lesser books of essays, *Travels on an Old Planet*. Eventually they settled on Venice. Monica disliked it, sensing a rot beneath the façade, but her mother wanted it, badly, and it was easier to give way than to fight. Still, Venice featured in her nightmares: she knew with sinking certainty she would end up there overseeing her mother's decline. Her hope was that she could keep that time as brief as possible within the bounds of decency.

But at last the subtext of her mother's messages became too pitiful, too clear. The increasingly limited activities, the friends whose names slipped away from her messages—at last, Monica couldn't put it off any longer. She found more or less what she expected—an old woman, rather frail, left behind by her set, her only companion a jenjer who was counting the hours until this episode of her bond came to an end and she could be released to some better, more stimulating task. Monica would not have wished such an end upon an enemy, and she did not, in fact, count her mother amongst her enemies.

Their household was luxurious, but life was very narrow and constrained, particularly given Monica's usual freedom. Her mother couldn't travel far and, by the end of the second year, was more or less bedridden. With nothing better to do, Monica wrote three novels, which she buried, and she put off a visit from the famous writer, who offered to remarry her. Occasionally she made it out into the wider world, but the company bored her, and the wonders of the old world did not astound: she knew that they were re-creations, fakes. She found herself looking more and more at the jenjer, wondering about them . . .

She wondered about them later, too, in Torello, these jenjer upon old Earth. What would be happening to them there, as news from the periphery came in? Rome had crucified six thousand, once upon a time, and the whole bloody planet was pockmarked with a hundred thousand gulags and plantations that over a hundred thousand years had kept the slaves oppressed. Had some of them taken flight, found their way beyond the periphery to . . . where? Some kind of haven? Some kind of training ground? But what about the ones left behind? What would happen to them when the war—and war was coming, that much was certain—when the war at last came? What would be done to them, and how far would they go to defend themselves? Lifting her eyes, Monica saw Gale, across the empty pool. She touched the tracker beneath her skin, pulsing away, without purpose.

. . .

Monica's mother took nearly three years, Earth years, to die. Frail and increasingly bedbound, her friends slipped away, one by one, until, at the end, there was only Lucy, obliged to be there in order to stay alive, and Monica, obliged to be there by ties so primal she sometimes wondered whether they could be called consensual.

The old woman's mind stayed sharp, and, listening to her talk (her mother liked conversation), Monica realised the specific gift that she had inherited from her mother—the gift for the telling detail. Her mother remade history to her own purposes—stories that Monica knew to be untrue in some respect were repeated over and over until they gained authenticity in her mother's mind or else, sometimes, were told unexpectedly in their true form, which Monica would realise, some hours later, had been an offering—an admission of guilt, perhaps, or a kind of apology for a moment missed, a mistake made. And the detail—ah, yes, the devil was there. The insult remembered in its entirety, down to a cruel mimicry of the cadences in which it was delivered; the inappropriateness of a rival's dress; and, sometimes, more touchingly, memories of great tenderness and love, of first seeing her husband-to-be; of the girl child's first word.

Tales from Torello were more limited: she talked about the death of her husband, casting it as a form of liberation. Leaving for the periphery had been an adventure at first, clearly, a way to shock her parents, but the reality had been bored exile, and, reading between the lines, Monica received validation of what she had often suspected over the years: how her mother had made her father's life there a misery. "It was better that he died," her mother said. "Better for you, too, able to leave that backwater and go to school at last . . ." Mostly she repeated this self-same story, over and over, but sometimes, more so towards the end, something would pop up that Monica had never heard before. Was it a form of confession? A bid to establish her version of events? Whatever the reason, something drove her to pass on information before the end.

She had one last sting in her tale. It was mid-morning, and Monica had been sitting by her bedside for a while, looking out of the big window across the water to St. Mark's and thinking how bizarre the reconstruction was, how strange to be sitting in a dead city on a dead world, brought artificially back to life, by a woman who was dying. Lucy was coming in and out, sorting bedlinen, tidying away the breakfast dishes, busy about the kinds of tasks with which she filled her day.

Monica, turning from the window, became aware that her mother was awake, and looking at her. Suddenly, her mother said, "Did you know what happened to the mayor?"

"I beg your pardon?"

"The mayor of Torello."

Monica hardly knew what to say. These were events from fifty years ago, at least; she could barely recall anything . . .

"He was murdered," her mother said.

"Murdered?"

"Oh yes. By his wife."

"Excuse me?"

"Don't use slang, Monica, it's terribly unbecoming."

"The mayor," Monica prompted.

"Yes, his wife. Killed him. Shot him dead late one night, through the head. That place, that dreadful place! I don't know why I ever went there."

"Wasn't his name Langley?"

"Yes, yes." Her mother's face softened in memory. "Oh, he was a handsome man! And she shot him in the face.

I liked him a great deal. He was a good friend of your father's, too."

Monica began to piece together little bits of overheard conversation, long forgotten; yes, she had known that the mayor had died, when she was quite small, but had certainly never worked out that it was murder. It was not the kind of thing her father would have discussed, and would not have figured in her mother's conversation either.

"We all knew that he hit her, of course," her mother went on. "The wives, I mean. We all knew. After it all happened, some of them wanted to testify on her behalf—but really, no. No. Langley was a big player on Sienna. Destroying his reputation would have given the Commonwealth the excuse to annex Sienna, and your father wasn't ready . . . Still too much bound up in Sienna; still not enough moved away. Anyway, I had a word here and a word there, and soon put a stop to that. It went to court and she was convicted."

"Did Daddy know about the mayor?"

"What was that, dear? Don't mutter—"

"Did Daddy know James Langley hit his wife?"

"I've no idea, darling." She sounded bored. "I doubt it. Women are good at hiding these things, if they want to. Most men don't know the half of it. I will say this about your father, I never felt any danger from him in that regard."

No, he had been a gentle man, in many ways.

"She asked me to speak to him," her mother said.

"Caroline Langley?"

"Mm. To your daddy. Ask for his help. I promised I would, but you see how I couldn't, don't you? Really, no. No. I told her that I had. Said that he'd told me to tell her he couldn't do anything."

The room was quiet. Outside the water of the lagoon lapped against the stone of the island, lapped and lapped, and ate away.

"What happened to her?" Monica said at last.

"To who?"

"The wife. The widow."

"Oh, what do they call it? The thing that they do . . ." She touched her wrist and her throat.

She was made jenjer. Suddenly, Monica became aware of Lucy, standing stock still at the far side of the room. She licked her lips and said, "And what happened to her bond?"

"Good heavens, Monica, I never asked! Hardly appropriate!" She closed her eyes. "I wonder, sometimes, what would have happened if I'd told your father . . ." She shook her head. "But no. No. He had too much to worry about. And the money—it wasn't safe yet. It wasn't off Sienna."

So he had given up, in the end, Monica thought. All

her wealth—why had she not considered this before? How easily she had gone from Sienna to the Commonwealth. He'd moved the money, just in time, just before everything he owned became worthless.

"You know, I thought I saw her again, just before we left," her mother said. "Impossible, of course. I don't know what they do with these people, but they don't just let them run around. Thank goodness."

Monica, conscious of Lucy, felt deep shame. The casualness with which their fates and destinies were discussed... She lowered her eyes, looked through her lashes at Lucy, as she gave her mother the pills, and that was how she caught the look of naked hatred on Lucy's face. Was this how all jenjer looked at us, Monica thought, when they think we are not looking?

The end came soon after, as if, with this tale told, her mother had nothing more to add to the story of her life. Over the next few weeks she withdrew into herself, remaining in bed, and rarely opening her eyes. Late one afternoon, almost asleep herself, Monica jolted awake, and saw her mother looking at her with sharp unvanquished eyes. That was the very last surge of life. She did not wake the following morning. Monica, coming in with breakfast, knew at once that her mother had gone. She sat for a while, holding the frail old hand, and pondering their lives together. She had not chosen this woman to be her mother and would not, truth be told, have chosen such a woman as her mother. Their bond had only ever worked one way, and she was not sorry to be free of it, although she was sad. Lucy came in, softly, and sized up the situation at once. Monica released her mother's hand.

"I'm sorry," Monica said.

Lucy stared at her. She had aged slowly, in the jenjer way, and now Monica had almost caught up with her.

"You were with her a long time," Monica said.

"Oh yes," said Lucy. "A very long time. The sights I've seen . . . We saw everything, you know," she said. "Witnessed everything. Justice. It was justice. And this—" She gestured round the lonely room. "Alone, rambling—this was justice too—"

"Stop now," Monica said, firmly. "She was my mother. I loved her."

"Justice," said Lucy. "We're coming. We're coming."

She paid off Lucy's bond and, as an added bonus, gave her the famous writer's first editions to sell. The woman was gone the following morning.

Where do they go to, these jenjer, Monica wondered, when they're free of us? Standing in Torello, she supposed she had her answer now. She had all the answers now.

Four

WAS IT HER? Monica wondered, staring into the empty pool. Did she come for revenge? The people of the town had kept her with her husband and, when at last she had broken free of him, colluded to punish her beyond what was reasonable. She had been trapped, friendless, and had come to her mother—and, so she thought, to her father—for aid. And she had been abandoned, and paid the ultimate penalty.

Who would not want revenge in those circumstances, Monica thought—and how glorious, how grand, how final. Torello burned; Sienna fallen; and Arthur Greatorex, whose task it was to protect her, shot dead knowing that his cause was lost.

"I could cry," said Monica to the night sky. "I could cry."

But for what? For her daddy, who had loved his home so much, but not enough to leave his money there? For her mother, who got everything she wanted from life? For herself, who had lived a good full life? Or for that woman, that jenjer—all jenjer—who would not, Monica suspected, want her tears.

She heard footsteps behind her. Turning, she saw Gale, and suddenly she was back, again, on the hillside, a girl not quite twelve years old, realising the depths of the danger she was in. She touched the tracker, which was throbbing still, uselessly, and Gale saw what she was doing and smiled.

"Where have you been?" she said.

"I walked up the hillside," he said. "There's an old up-link there."

"I know. Is it working?"

He took a step towards her. He could kill her now, and nobody would ever know. Nobody would care. Soon there would be war, and there would be a great many dead bodies.

"I got it working again," he said. "You can go, if you want, although I don't think we'll be able to persuade someone to come and collect you."

"No," she said. "It's much too late for that."

"You should have gone when you had the chance."

"I wasn't ready. I didn't understand . . ."

"And now?"

"Now," she said, "I think I understand."

"Do you?" He moved towards her, swift, silent, catlike. "Do you really?"

"Justice," she said.

"Not only that."

"Yes, of course. Retribution."

He sighed at the word, like a thirsty man thinking of a cool drink. "You might want to be somewhere else when we arrive."

"But there isn't anywhere else, is there?" she said, her words tumbling out. "People can run, but there's nowhere to hide. Not the core worlds, not old Earth. You're everywhere."

"Yes," he said. "We're everywhere. In your blood and in your bones."

"Will there be some kind of signal, when the time comes?"

"I don't know," he said, and then corrected himself. "I don't know yet."

"Do you hate us so much?"

He looked at her steadily. "Yes."

"Do you hate me, Gale?"

He contemplated her for a few moments, his eyes bright and unblinking. At last, he said, "You were always very kind."

Yes, she thought, he hates me.

He turned to go. "Come or go as you please, Monica," he said. "But we're coming."

He disappeared into the darkness. Yes, they were coming, and the war was coming with them. They are coming, the slaves that we made, she thought, and we made them powerful and relentless, and their memories long and precise.

She looked around. Where could she go? Back to the core? Why? What was the point? She might as well stay here, see them when they came . . .

She laughed. And why not? Why not? Yes, she thought, she would stay. She would watch them come.

She went inside and began work. Her old style came back, easily, learned decades ago and finessed over years. They were coming, and she would see them come. She would observe from the front lines, as she always had done, and send back news of everything she sees, send out her signal into the coming storm.

Acknowledgments

Huge thanks to Marco Palmieri, who took a single-sentence Twitter pitch and said, "We should do that . . . send me an outline." My thanks also to Lee Harris for nurturing this project through the last stages to publication.

I'm very grateful to the librarian at Newnham College, Cambridge, who let me perch in the library for months. That is where this story was written. And, as ever, I am in debt to Matthew, who does all the heavy lifting while I sit in libraries living my best life.

About the Author

UNA MCCORMACK is a *New York Times* bestselling author and a university lecturer in creative writing. She has written novels, short stories, and audio dramas for franchises such as Star Trek, Doctor Who, and Blake's 7. She lives in Cambridge, England, with her partner and their daughter. They have no cats and one Dalek.

TOR · COM

Science fiction. Fantasy. The universe.

And related subjects.

*

More than just a publisher's website, *Tor.com*
is a venue for **original fiction, comics,** and
discussion of the entire field of SF and fantasy,
in all media and from all sources. Visit our site
today—and join the conversation yourself.